One 'n Done #9

W(h)ine and Cheese

by

S. Atzeni

Published by

Read: [*v*] The act of interpreting and understanding language, symbols, and the written word.

Furiously: [*adv*] To do something with excitement and passion.

Read Often. Read Well.
Read Furiously

- The End -

It is a truth universally acknowledged that a college student, in possession of an attentive audience of their friends, will make this all about them.

~Jane Austen (maybe)

The day Mal broke up with me, I thought about trees. We were inside the Student Center, which is a strange place to look for them; plants don't do well in this environment. The Center is a giant collection of random places, events, and people: a food court, couches filled with sleeping students using the school newspapers for blankets, rooms on the second floor meant to be used for events but sit silently most days (unless someone can get the room open, then everyone uses it for a quiet study space until we're kicked out), student organization offices, and a very unhelpful help desk because being a student worker means you are getting paid minimum wage to do your homework. The entire building is made up of rectangular windows that fit from floor to ceiling, allowing us glimpses of the outside world as we study our life away, but also toasting us quite thoroughly if one sits too close (or falls asleep on the couches - you don't want that kind of sunburn). On good days, the sun holds us close in its gentle embrace. On bad days, it glares at us with a fire of a thousand…um, suns? Oh crap, this got away from me.

The very big windows also give you a beautiful view of campus, but can be a bit jarring as birds tend to fly into them, the *thunk thunk* sound of their tiny bodies hitting the glass as they fall to the ground (it's a long way to the bottom) ruin the navel-gazing that college students have perfected for centuries. It's very hard to keep one's head up one's ass when you've just witnessed avian homicide.

So it wasn't an actual tree I was thinking of when I was being dumped, but the idea of a tree. Semiotically speaking, I was thinking of the socio-cultural meaning centered on the word "tree" rather than the physical representation of it. Which then led me to consider that when I think of the word "tree," why do I think of those childlike drawings of trees? You know the ones: the brown rectangle with big green, loopy-loops imitating what? Branches? Leaves? Both? Why have we normalized this idea that leaves and/or the tops of trees are curly or twisted lines of green? I drew so many of those trees and everyone - parents, teachers, most grown-ups - applauded my artistic ability to (not) capture a physical representation of the tree. Instead we were encouraged to continue to look like assholes as we drew these brown rectangles with curly hair on top. Don't get me started on the hole in the center of this supposed "tree." Seriously, were the adults laughing at us behind our five-year-old backs? "That'll show them," they cackled to each other, helping themselves to another plate of Entenmann's coffee cake. "That'll show them for thinking the world cares." So we continued to draw these abominations of the botanical community: brown rectangle, gaping hole in the center, and unruly tops that resembled nothing related to photosynthesis.

"Are you listening to me?" Mal demanded, narrowing their eyes.

"What? Yes, I am," I lied. "You were trying to break up with me."

"I'm not *trying* to do anything," Mal said. "I *am* breaking up with you. This isn't working. We've been having -"

As Mal continued to break up with me, I thought of the concept of trees and the lack thereof of their physical manifestations. I think the beauty surrounding being a college student means you are allowed a space where you can be this pretentious, so I wasn't about to squander this privilege. Thus, I allowed myself to consider the conceptual framework of trees. Bits of what Mal was trying to say were breaking through; however, my hyperfocus continued to protect me from what was happening directly in front of me. *I'm winning!* I crowed delightedly to myself as I won a competition no one else entered. *I'm winning the breakup moment by refusing to pay attention!*

Over Mal's shoulder, I stared at the student flag for the Environmental Club. My roommate Ana and I started it after we noticed our small liberal arts college had the big student organizations - student newspaper, Greek life, sports, cultural organizations - but no club devoted to making sure we all didn't die in a horrible climate change disaster. When we presented the application to the student government, they looked at us with a mix of sadness and pity. "You can try," the student government president told us, "But no one wants to think about this during their free time." Naturally, our undeserved youthful confidence told us that this particular student government president, as a senior, had been broken by the college system. Obviously, we were much smarter than this senior. We will change the world with our kindness, brilliance, and altruism.

Unfortunately, no one else saw it our way. The first meeting, and every one since, have consisted of two members: the president/ vice president (Ana) and the secretary/treasurer/event coordinator (me). It's a lot easier than it sounds. We don't have enough members for a budget, so there isn't even a treasury and/or events to organize. Super easy! Our first, and only, order of business was to create the student flag. This is the flag that hangs in the Center and is on display to showcase all of the extraordinary things happening at the college. *See?* The flags say to tour groups. *Our students are better than all the other students out there! Your mediocre child will also get this unearned confidence if they apply here!* Of course, Ana and I were told it wasn't necessary to have a flag since there weren't enough members, but we insisted. Because it was for Mother Earth, after all. Plus we wanted to be included when the tour groups bring the prospective students around to feel bad about the lack of extra curricular activities.

Mal continued to drone on about something. "I just feel all of our fighting is taking its toll…be best if we…I'm sorry it went on for so long…I think it's better if…"

Anyway, the flag was felt on felt on felt, depicting a cartoon child standing in front of its parent. We didn't have the artistic talent - or enough felt - for any features, but it clearly showcases human forms because we made sure to give them heads, bodies, arms, and legs. We tried to angle the child's head toward the parent, but we couldn't get the neck right so there's extra felt covering all of the extra glue that came about during this process. Also, in felt, are the words "Daddy, Mommy, what are trees?" and one lone, small tree in the background (it didn't occur to us that including the tree established a logical fallacy. In felt). We understand there is only one felt parent in front of the inquisitive felt child, so it seems strange that the child is talking to both parents. However, we ran out of felt, so we decided the question should be an interpretative one. Yet also literal. And also rhetorical. And also thought-provoking.

And yes, it looks *exactly* like you think it would.

How provocative! We applauded ourselves. *Yes, felt child, what* are *trees? For you will never know, will you? As we progress on this landscape of terror-filled environmental changes! If only your parents had an environmental club during their college years, they would be able to stop you from living in a treeless world!*

Tears sprang to my eyes as I stared at our student

flag. *This felt child will never draw a stupid looking tree, I thought. It will never know where to put the curly bits.*

Mal, mistaking my tears for their breakup speech, reached for my hand. "Hey, Ains," Mal said softly. "I still care about you."

Too late, I finally realized what was happening. "Are you breaking up with me?!" I screeched a bit too loudly. A few students rustled under their newspapers.

Mal's face clouded over with confusion. "Y-y-yes," Mal stammered. "That's what this is about."

"Wait!" I said. "I'm not ready! Go back to the beginning!" Frantically, I searched around for the Environmental Club's flag, but, in my panic, I couldn't locate it. It was gone. Like the trees.

"Go back?" Mal repeated. Now they really looked concerned. "Are you okay?"

"No, I'm not okay!" I snapped. "You are breaking up with me. On a *Wednesday*. Why are you doing this?"

Again, Mal looked at me. "I just spent fifteen minutes telling you why." Frustrated, they stood up. "I'm done. This is why. Because we're not on the same level."

"And what level is that?" I said. "The level where you want to break up with me and I don't want you to? This is insane!"

Now in their coat and backpack, Mal looked down at me where I was sitting. "No, Ainsley, it's not," Mal said. "I told you all the reasons why this isn't working. I'm going to class now." As they turned to go, Mal said over their shoulder - *over their shoulder*, dear reader! As though the conversation was over and I knew where we stood! But I wasn't *listening*! - "I hope we can still be friends."

Ugh. There it was. I wanted to say, "No, Mal. We cannot still be friends because I am clearly surprised by all of this" but that would require me to admit what I had been thinking about this entire time. And it wasn't my relationship's demise.

Didn't anyone care about these fucking trees?

******

After Mal left, I sat on the couch and stared out the big windows of the Student Center. Only two birds crashed into the windows in the three hours I sat there. I sat there for so long, I missed Greek Mythology. I knew I should do something that resembled a responsible college student, so I took out my phone and sent in my standard "I feel sick today" email.

Twenty minutes later, I received a reply from my professor. "Please feel better," read the email. "Today in class we discussed Daphne and her unfortunate fate. For the next class, write a brief response on this myth and what it would be like to become a tree. Best wishes!"

Oh, Daphne, you have no idea what will happen to you one day, I thought. Looking up, I finally spotted our flag again. *Daddy, Mommy, what are trees?* The tears began all over again.

I'm not sure how long I sat there, feeling sorry for myself. I also felt sorry for the trees, but most of my pity was reserved for myself. It was definitely long enough for my roommates to come looking for me. Ana and Padma were rounding the corner of the expansive couch section of the Center when they finally spotted me.

"Finally!" Ana said when they reached my couch. "Where have you been?"

"You weren't in Greek Mythology today," Padma added. "Are you okay?"

Looking at them, I burst into tears. Again. "Mal

broke up with me," I sobbed.

Immediately, my dear and wonderful friends flew to my side to capture me in a group hug. "Oh, sweetie, I'm so sorry," Padma said. Padma was our resident Dorm Mom, who was always ready to offer "sweetie" or "honey" in comfort, provide chicken soup for our dejected souls, and make sure we washed our clothes during finals week. As the oldest child of five, Padma was used to taking care of pathetic, helpless creatures, so she thrived as the Dorm Mom, where she could be both hero and martyr. "Did they say why?"

"Yes," I managed to choke out. "But I wasn't paying attention and I don't knowwwwwww!" That last part stretched out as I let out another sob.

Ana and Padma pulled away simultaneously. "Wait, what?" Ana said. She narrowed her eyes, considering whether she should take back her sympathy. Like me, Ana was a child of immigrants and she didn't take too kindly to people or situations that wasted her precious time. We had too much we had to do - too many generations of dreams to accomplish in four short years. I can already see the thoughts forming in her head: *is this a real problem or an Ainsley problem?* I overheard Padma and Ana say that once. While I wasn't sure what the context is for an "Ainsley problem," the term left its mark. Now my paranoia of what they were discussing that day has spilled over into me struggling to ask or accept any help from my roommates.

The words came out fast. "Mal was talking about it while I looked out the window and I wanted to listen but I didn't and then when they were finished, there was no Q and A and now it's over!" I reached for my friends, but they stayed where they were. Ana and Padma stared at me warily, not quite sure how best to proceed.

Finally, Padma broke the silence. "Are you happy or sad about this?" Padma asked.

"What? I'm sad!" I exclaimed. "That's why I'm crying!"

"What were you thinking about?" Ana asked. "What was so important outside that you couldn't pay attention?"

Here it goes. I took a deep breath. "Trees," I whispered.

The silence was long. The silence was uncomfortable. The silence was incredulous. Padma and Ana looked at me, then at each other, and then - for good measure - outside where the trees were swaying their leaves majestically in a dance that *does not resemble a top of curly hair. It just doesn't.* I shifted uncomfortably, watching my upper hand in this conversation fade away. *Daddy, Mommy, where is Ainsley's credibility?*

Before I could defend myself, Padma and Ana burst out laughing. Not a cute little giggle, but like two witches in Hades cackling about Daphne's new situation. They grabbed their sides and gasped for air. I glared at them. "Is something funny?" I asked.

Ana tried to speak, but couldn't make the words. Instead she rolled off the couch and onto the floor, this time laughing *and* crying (honestly, dearest reader isn't that a bit much?). Padma tried to regain some composure. "You are the only person I know that thinks of trees while being dumped," she said. Ana snorted in response. They exchanged glances with each other and the phrase reappeared: *it's an Ainsley problem.* I tried to swallow my panic at losing any sympathy for what I'm assuming is an upsetting situation for most people.

I huffed, in an attempt to regain my higher ground once more. "Laugh it up. One day the trees will be gone and children will have to ask what they are."

That stopped them. They soberly looked in the direction of the Environmental Club's student flag. They stared at the felt child and its rhetorical question. "Well, shit," Ana said.

*****

I guess you can say that I overreacted. I wouldn't say that, but people who are terrible at feeling their emotions or hate love could say that.

Let me preface that it wasn't as if I didn't care that Mal was trying to dump me. My moment of disassociation was brought on by the unpleasantness of our last few weeks. College relationships are very delicate ecosystems. Since you are always around each other, share similar social circles, and/or have free time outside of studying and small part-time jobs, college relationships evolve quicker than relationships in the real world. They also become very dependent on their environment, making it very difficult to disentangle when the relationship no longer serves the people in it. Those involved - the couple, the friends, the innocent bystanders sleeping under student newspaper-blankets - are suddenly involved, whether they want to be or not. While I was upset that my relationship ended, the added humiliation that other people were witness to it, student flags and dead birds included, and the new normal of not following the already-agreed upon ritual of hanging out after class, eating meals together, and having weekends already planned out added to my disorientation. In short, I was upset with having to find a new normal on top of the many other responsibilities I was supposed to be doing.

Mal and I had the same major and took the same classes. We connected the first day we met because we had so much in common. In the real world, we know there is more to a relationship than that, but in the rosy world of collegiate codependence, it was all we needed. It seemed like fate that we were always together rather than the dedicated algorithm established for all majors via Records and Registration. The longer we stayed together, the more difficult it was for anyone in our social circle to see us as two different people. Suddenly, if you wanted to speak to one of us, it didn't matter which one because the other person was standing right there. No one assumed we would have separate interests or separate plans - "Mal-and-Ains" became the simplistic, catchall name to refer to us. Similar to being a celebrity couple, but without the adulation that makes it all worthwhile.

Any biologist will tell you that environments need to adapt in order to sustain themselves. Granted, we had many biology majors on campus, but none in my social circle, so we did not know this. As a result, "Mal-and-Ains," being English majors, began to act out their very own poor adaptation of *Who's Afraid of Virginia Woolf?* With the resentment of two people forced together, our arguing went from everyday tiffs to elaborate scenes where we refused to yield the stage as we strode back and forth, trading what we believed were witty barbs. Instead, they were thinly veiled insults, hiding a strong vitriol for each other, leaving our captive audience feeling very uncomfortable.

In light of all this, I knew something was coming. But if I was being honest, I just wasn't in the mood to deal with it at that moment. It felt easier to dedicate my emotional bandwidth to a problem I couldn't fix - the devastating effects of climate change and the loss of plant life in the coming decades - rather than a problem that was in front of me for weeks.

Of course, part of me was relieved that it was over and also relieved that I didn't have to be the bad person in all this. Now I can rightfully blame Mal for destroying the ecosystem while I take my place as the person scorned. With the aftermath on its way as people began asking questions, I accepted this instant gratification in the form of a pity party, self-destructive behaviors, and (my personal favorite) the egocentric high road.

*****

My conflicting feelings created a lot of problems in the weeks following the breakup. One minute I obviously didn't care, but the next I was making sure everyone did. It didn't matter that I couldn't remember the actual event or what was said; I needed proof from everyone that I had been wronged.

As this was my first "real-ish" relationship, no one told me that there was an expiration date on how long I could play the victim. I honestly thought it would be like *Cats* - I could perform this role, making it a staple to my very identity. But like *Cats*, the schtick got old really fast and I was beginning to lose what little legitimacy I had left. I was also running the risk of having this situation go from worthwhile cultural significance to a hastily thrown together event, making people uncomfortable with how straightforward it was toward cat anuses.

That delicate ecosystem, and the college students that live within it, hate change. So imagine my surprise when Mal showed up to breakfast the next day, bringing their tray over to sit at our usual table.

"Um, what do you think you're doing?" I demanded as they dropped their bag on the floor.

"Eating breakfast before our Poetry Seminar," Mal answered, looking confused.

"You can't sit here with us anymore," I said. "We're 'broken up,' remember?" I used air quotes since this is what allegedly happened.

"Okay, and?" Mal asked. They looked around the table for confirmation, stopping on Ana and Padma.

I smiled smugly. *My roommates get it*, I thought. *They won't let this tree-hating monster get away with it.*

Ana and Padma looked down at their pancakes. "Um, well," Padma muttered, "we're all still friends, right?"

"What?" I shouted. A bit too loudly for breakfast.

"We are most certainly not friends!" I turned to Mal. "You made that clear yesterday. When you 'broke up' with me." I used more air quotes to make my point.

"Ains, come on," Mal said. "We can be adults about this."

"Ugh," I said. "Don't do that. Don't take the 'moral high ground' with me."

"Okay, enough with the air quotes," Ana said.

"Well, I'm just trying to make sense of this," I said. "First, I am *humiliated* in the Student Center. Then, I am supposed to just be okay with having breakfast with the person who apparently thinks they're too good to date me?"

"That isn't what I said!" Mal protested.

"Oh, it isn't?" I asked. "Well, then, Mal, please tell everyone here what it was you actually said to me."

Mal took a deep breath. *This is it!* I thought triumphantly. *Mystery solved!* Mal turned to my roommates. "I feel bad saying this, but here it is: as you know, Ains and I have not been getting along lately." They nodded to Padma. "You remember our conversation from last week, right?"

The blood rushed from my face. This wasn't going the way I thought it would. Wait - so now everyone is getting together to talk about me? And Padma knew about this?

Padma nodded. "Yes, I remember," she said. "I'm glad I was able to help."

"Help with what?" I demanded. I pushed my breakfast tray away, suddenly feeling sick. "What did you two talk about?"

Padma got quiet again and looked down at her tray. It was suddenly very important that she cut up her strawberries just so.

"Anyway," Mal continued. "After your advice, I thought about what I needed to do for myself and that's when I decided to let Ains know how I was feeling." At this point, Mal turned to me. "I didn't mean for it to come out that way," (*fuuuuuck! I should have paid more attention yesterday*) "but I'm really glad I got to speak my truth."

"What the fuck is happening?" I asked. I felt light-headed. Am I being dumped twice within 24 hours?

"Ains," Mal said, taking my hand. Ana and Padma, playing excellent versions of coed Judases, leaned forward to listen. "Ains," Mal said again. "I appreciate that you understand how mismatched we are. I think I just needed someone to connect with when I transferred here in the fall. Our time together was really important in getting me acclimated to my new surroundings, but I think it's time for me to really consider what I want in a partner."

"So, let me get this straight," I said slowly. "You didn't really like me - you just felt like the new kid and needed to make a friend? And then, what, one thing led to another?" I turned to Padma. "And then Mal confided this 'truth' (*now a great use for air quotes!*) to you and your 'advice' (*yes! Two for two!*) to Mal was to dump me and find a more suitable partner?" I looked across the table. "Did I get that right?"

Padma didn't look up from her fruit. "Not quite, but sort of," she mumbled.

Realizing that Padma was struggling to not look terrible in all this, Ana jumped in. "I think Padma was trying to be a friend to both of you," she said. "We were both concerned at how much you were fighting, and I think we should applaud Mal for taking the initiative so both of you can be happy."

"What?!" I screeched. Definitely a bit too loudly for breakfast. "You are applauding Mal?! The person who dumped me? The person who used me to make friends?!" I gripped the table trying to stay focused on the cool surface before my rage made me pass out. I could feel my breathing starting to speed up.

Then it happened.

The three of them shared a look. It was practiced and it said exactly what I feared: *this is an Ains problem.* I stood up, feeling dizzy. "Thanks for being so honest, *friends,*" I said, choking the words out. "Mal, since we're so cool now, take notes for me in Poetry Sem because I'm going to lie down."

And so began my post-breakup anger. One minute you think you're going to be a person scorned (after being dumped in a Student Center) and the next you're being dumped (again) by not one but three people you care about. One breakup a person can handle, but three breakups? It can complicate your entire day.

Later that day, Ana and Padma tried to apologize and explain themselves, but I didn't feel like listening. For the next four weeks, I made sure my schedule didn't overlap with theirs. I went to breakfast earlier and stayed at the library later in the evenings. I sat in the back of class so I didn't have to look directly at Mal and/or be forced to engage in conversation when it was time to circle up (as is a major requirement for all Humanities majors - stare awkwardly at your peers as you bullshit about the book you didn't read).

It took me four weeks of this avoidance to realize that no one was going to change this delicate college ecosystem. Everyone still remained friends and it seemed everyone was just patiently waiting for me to "get over it." For some reason that fueled my anger and I added an additional two weeks to my own sentence. At the end of this principled statement (that made sense only to me), my brother decided to weigh in.

My brother Jason was two years older than me and belonged to the least popular fraternity on campus. It could be because, unlike the other Greek life on campus, his fraternity was filled with the awkward nerds who were rejected by the more popular groups. It also didn't help that his Greek letters, Tau Rho Delta, spelled out TRD. They were literal turds on the Greek life hierarchy. What I always admired about my brother is that nothing gets him down - even if he's walking around with TRD emblazoned across his chest.

"Okay, we need to talk," Jason said one morning. I

was going on six weeks of eating breakfast with Jason and his brothers. Understanding what it means to be cast out by their peers, they welcomed me at an earlier breakfast time. At first they respectfully allowed me to mope about and wax poetically on the decline of our world, but after a while, even their charity began to wane.

"About what?" I said warily. Was this group going to reject me too? How much lower is rock bottom?

"You need to apologize to Ana and Padma," Jason said. His brothers nodded in agreement.

"No," I said simply. "Was that it?"

"Ains," Jason said patiently. "You can't do this. Trust me, soon your time here will be over and you'll look back and realize you wasted time being mad over nothing."

"It's something to *me*," I said. "They betrayed me."

"Betrayed you?" Lunch Box repeated. ""Did you even ask them to explain their side of the story?"

"I didn't have to," I said. "They gave each other *the look*."

"What look?" Jason asked. So I had to explain, in humiliating detail, about "the Ains problem" and what I feared happened every time I left the room. Jason and his brothers listened intently until I was finished. "Ains, if you were so difficult to be around, why would they be friends with you?" Jason asked. "This is a pretty big school."

"I don't know," I said. "Maybe for the same reason Mal only dated me because they just transferred in?"

"Okay, real talk," Lunch Box cut in. "I hate to say it -"

"No, you don't," Trash Bag interrupted. Lunch Box silenced him with a look of his own.

"Okay, I don't hate to say it," Lunch Box said. "Mal was gross."

Jason and his brothers nodded in agreement. "They really are," Jason agreed. "Mal was always talking about making it big in the indie music scene. Mal can't even play an instrument. Or sing."

"And correcting everyone on their literary criticism responses," added E.K. (short for Electric Kettle). "I hated taking American Naturalism with Mal last fall."

"And you didn't like Mal either," Jason added. "I think you liked the idea of Mal, but not really Mal."

I sat quietly, considering their take. Amidst these

TRDs with their kitchen-based nicknames, I realize they may be right. "Do you think my ego got in the way of this break-up?" I ventured, reveling in my well-placed epiphany that I reached entirely on my own with no help from this conversation.

To my horror, I was met with a resounding *yes*. (I would have taken a bit of protest - *what ego, Ains? Honestly, you are the most down-to-Earth person I met! You're so stable - like a tree!*) They didn't even consider it, those stupid TRD brothers. But it was my actual brother who left me with a final thought: "Oh definitely. You are also the worst. Which is why it worked for so long."

*****

I'll spare you the tearful apologies, dear reader, but there were many. Ana and Padma tried to explain that they weren't siding with Mal, but really liked us together separately. I wasn't a fan of this logic, as it still felt very pointed, but I tried to ignore images of *the look* and pressed on with the thought that we were all friends.

Right?

I didn't have too much time to consider the complicated questions that plague the evolution of friendship because, well, midterms. Being the well-mannered, Type-A students that we have been since the roles were forced upon us in childhood, we quickly resolved all moments of human interaction in favor of spending long sessions of silent contemplation and anxiety-building in the library study rooms. Naturally, I made sure to hide whenever Mal joined a study session and spent a good portion of my midterm preparation in the creepy library basement with old editions of JSTOR to keep me company. I tried not to think about how my roommates welcomed Mal into their study groups with open arms and instead reminded myself that all has been forgiven and we were all moving on. I needed to play my part well in this ecosystem.

After (sort of) passing (most) of my midterms, we began to play the very complicated game of let's-make-every-moment-count-because-the-semester-is-almost-over and please-keep–away-from-me-I-am-failing-two-of-my-classes-and-the-semester-is-almost-over. Mal found someone else to dazzle with their lack of musical ability and overinflated sense of self-importance. Soon their presence in our friend group began to wane until one day, it was as though Mal never existed. Ana and Padma noted this with a disinterest that would have enraged me if I didn't, as I mentioned many times before, moved on from the experience.

BUT.

If I *hadn't* moved on - as I mentioned already - I probably *would have* pointed out that Mal's lack of loyalty to our friend group, dropped at the first sign of spring and a new relationship, exhibited the poor qualities of a friend that should not be included in *said friend group*. In addition, all of this strife with those *who are still in this particular friend group* could have been avoided if *this particular friend group* listened to the person who was on the receiving end of the breakup and removed Mal from *this particular friend group* immediately after this *particular breakup event*.

In other words, I had moved on, so I didn't feel the need to shout: was it worth it to take Mal's side over mine? Was it worth it to make me look overly emotional and unstable when Mal couldn't be bothered to text and say that they weren't coming to breakfast, lunch, or dinner ever again? Do you see what I put up with all this time?

It is so fortunate, dear reader, that I had moved on! We certainly saved ourselves a lot of trouble!

*****

Father, Mother, What Are Trees?: An Academic Reading of the Mythology of Daphne

It is very interesting to think about Daphne and the context of trees, especially within the confines of Greek mythology, a mythology that has been around since the beginning of society and humanity. It is also very interesting to think about this story because Daphne is turned into a tree, thus making it a story about Daphne's escape and the importance of trees. In this paper, I will discuss the importance of trees and also explain why Daphne's story is important to readers, historians, and this class.

To begin, firstly, Daphne became a tree after she asked her father, the river god, to save her from Apollo's advances. Apollo is obviously in the wrong here because his toxic masculinity reminds us that people cannot just decide when a relationship starts and finishes. Also, can we discuss Daphne's terrible friends who allowed this behavior to continue rather than stepping in and taking Daphne's side when it is obvious that Daphne is the victim here? Please note I use "victim" in a traditional sense as per the mythological time period, and am only applying it to Daphne rather than someone else who also struggled with a toxic relationship, but is in fact, thriving in their current situation. Daphne, however, is a tree.

Secondly, Daphne was transformed into a laurel tree, which is a very significant tree in Greek mythology. A laurel tree is known as an evergreen tree, meaning it is constantly beloved and would never be criticized openly by the other trees in the forest because in an arboreal environment, being considered a "classic personality" still means something. It is a positive attribute that trees do not have social media, as the laurel tree's evergreen status would drop significantly once other trees started to post lies about what happened during certain breakup events (i.e. Apollo). It is unclear to scientists and classics scholars today whether or not trees have friendships and/or relationships; however, it is important to understand that Daphne was a person first and if some trees contain persons, then this would be the case.

Thirdly, laurel wreaths are part of laurel trees and are symbols of victory, particularly in the Olympics, which are also Greek. Ironically, but not, the laurel wreath is a symbol of Apollo which is another example of how people take and take without any understanding that others, like Daphne, also contributed to the narrative, but are now seen as too dramatic because Apollo got to everyone first. The laurel wreath should not be confused with the olive branch, which no one offered me. Or Daphne.

In conclusion, I would not like to be a tree because I feel there are too many stipulations around the best way to move on from your previous life into your tree life. One minute you can reminisce about the old days when you were a human and were happy, and the next the trees in your forest are telling you that you are in your tree phase now and it's time to move on. Which I did as did Daphne. Also, with the way climate change is moving through the globe, trees will just wither and die anyway. So once again, Daphne got the literal shit end of the tree branch.

Ains, what a magnificent, passionate reading of this myth! As your reader, I was floored by your commitment to pathos and kairos - both of which contributed to the tone of this paper. However, I feel this paper could do with another draft, as it does not quite fit into our class discussion and does not contain any secondary sources, which are important to synthesize your ideas with the course material. The casual language and run-on sentences also affected the academic reading of this argument.

As you revise this paper, I encourage you to keep to the readings and focus your analysis on the myth of Daphne and Apollo rather than the universal reading of relationships.

I will be happy to connect during office hours to discuss a rewrite.

(Also, I hope all is well with you. Please don't give any thought to what other "trees" think is the proper way to be a tree. Be your own tree.)

~ Professor A.

*****

After leaving my professor's office hours, I decided to take the long way back to my dorm. Our campus is really quite beautiful with its massive amount of trees. Plus I wanted to be alone. The weather was beginning to warm up, so a few students were studying outside. But it wasn't spring quite yet and the students were wearing their puffy winter coats and hats, looking like very collegiate penguins.

I wasn't sure what it means to "be my own tree," but I walked through the brisk, almost-spring weather feeling renewed. I looked forward to having this rewrite assignment to distract me.

As I turned the corner, I stopped short when I noticed Mal and their new group of friends. The new relationship absorbed Mal almost immediately into its social ecosystem and I was going on almost two weeks without a sighting. In a panic, I ducked into the Student Center.

The door I chose was the back of the Center where I reported to work as a student office worker. The offices were closed today, so the only people there were the poor souls that were trying to get students to sign up for petitions or volunteer opportunities. College students refuse to add more to their already-crammed plate of school, drama, and socializing, making this a worthless cause. The dimly lit hallway added to the soulless aesthetic, which is exactly what I needed to hide from a potential social interaction.

"Excuse me?" someone said behind me. I turned around, fearing the worst. Luckily, it was a person I never met before.

"Yes?" I said.

"Do you have a moment to discuss why the school should compost the leftover food in the food halls?" the person asked.

"I do not," I answered. "But thanks."

"Wait," this person said. "Please stand here and pretend to listen. I haven't gotten a signature all day." They gestured to their table. "We have stickers."

I glanced at the table. Most of the stickers were shouting at me - a bit too enthusiastically - about how important it is to save the environment.

Go green!

Compost or bust!

Make trees, not waste!

Feed the worms! (in a non creepy way)

"These are truly horrible," I said.

The person huffed. "At least they aren't as ridiculous as that tree flag."

Now it was my turn to get huffy. "That flag is provocative, rhetorical, and heart-wrenching."

"Did you make the flag?" they asked.

"I may have contributed to it."

"My condolences, I'm Quinn, by the way. I'm with the Gardening Club."

"There's a Gardening Club?" I said. "Since when?"

"Since I realized we don't have a club that encourages conservation and environmental strategies for the future," Quinn said.

"Um, we have one of those," I snapped. "It's the Environmental Club."

"Isn't that, like, two people?" Quinn said.

Ugh. A good point. "And?"

"Well, maybe we can join forces. Our club only has five people" (show-off) "and with your two, we might almost have actual organization numbers."

"Funding would be nice," I conceded. "Felt is really expensive."

"What?" Quinn said.

"Forget it," I said. "I'm Ains."

"So did you come this way to support your fellow students who are stupid enough to volunteer in the sign-up hallway?" Quinn said.

"Not at all," I said. "I'm hiding from my ex."

"Sorry to hear that," Quinn said.

"Don't be," I said. "To be honest, I don't remember the breakup, so it isn't that big of a deal." At Quinn's confused look, I explained the entire story. To my surprise, Quinn burst out laughing. I don't know if it was a new person hearing the story or that time heals (most) wounds, but I laughed with Quinn, feeling as though I was finally in on the joke. It felt good to laugh without the added baggage of worrying what everyone else was thinking.

"That is the best story I've ever heard," Quinn said. "If I'm being honest, you have the right idea."

"I do?" I asked.

"Absolutely," Quinn said. "If someone tries to break up with you, just think about that creepy weird flag you made. It puts everything in perspective."

"How so?" I asked.

"Because it reminds us that things could always be worse," Quinn said. "I mean the flag, not just the environmental destruction."

I laughed. "Creating felt people is really hard to do!" I said. "I don't see *your* club creating a flag to hang up."

"Of course not," Quinn said. "Obviously, the best environmental message was already taken."

We grinned at each other. "Well," I said. "I'm glad you know that true art can't be improved upon."

"Exactly," Quinn said. "Thanks to you, I now know the importance of trees." Quinn glanced at the clock overhead. "Hey, I'm going to head out. Do you want to get something to eat?"

I considered this. Normally any new people were vetted by the entire friend group, making sure this person fit all the personalities. Even dating felt like a team sport. But I really liked the idea of having someone all to myself, even just for a little while.

"Sure," I said.

- The Middle -

"It was the best of times, it was the worst of times, it was the misuse of cheese, it was the age of foolishness, it was the unbelievable lack of wine, it was the epoch of awkwardness, it was the season of fights, it was the season of pettiness, it was the spring of hope, it was almost the end of the semester."

- definitely not Charles Dickens

The first Frisbee went unnoticed. The second Frisbee went a little noticed, but nothing came of it. The third, fourth, and fifth Frisbee started to raise some questions.

Jason had been tasked with the title of "social chair," (meaning, in theory, he was responsible for the kegs whenever they threw a party), but, like me, my brother needed constant validation from his peers. So he decided to "class" up his "reign as social chair." (I put these words in quotation marks because I really need you to understand, dear reader, that I would never say anything that stupid. Also, it is very important to always cite one's source). The plan was to throw the most exciting party the student body has ever seen, but a few factors were standing in the way of a great party, therefore holding Jason back from his legacy of TRD social chair:

1. No one cared remotely about socializing with TRDs

2. As college students, parties were means to an end and making them too complicated would definitely be a disaster

3. As the lowest on the Greek life hierarchy,

> Jason wasn't working with too much of a budget
4. In fact, there wasn't a budget
5. Okay, that's not true. Jason had $12 to spend as he saw fit

If you put together these factors, anyone with sense would just go back to the tried and true method of throwing a party where the house got trashed and everyone got drunk. However, my brother refused to be deterred from what he felt was a necessary part of everyone's college experience: Jason's great, "classy" idea was none other than a wine and cheese party (ahem, experience).

According to the O.G. of party-planning, Martha Stewart, a wine and cheese party is considered an easy, relaxing way to mingle with friends, engage in great conversation, and snack on delectable small plates, most of which contain cheese. Wine must be paired appropriately with the dishes. By choosing the best red or white wine to complement your cheese, you ensure a delicious and exciting flavor profile for your guests. Paired with lovely home decor, music that is classic, yet upbeat, yet blends into the background, and multiple opportunities to mingle throughout a myriad of spaces - kitchen, living room, dining room, sitting room, basically any room that looks like *HGTV Magazine* threw up in it - the essence of a wine and cheese party is an excellent way to toast your good fortunes and your future as friends.

Of course, Jason knew none of this. I realized as much when he asked if I could accompany him to the dollar store to get supplies for the upcoming party. I agreed because this mess was too good to pass up and my social calendar had been considerably empty over these last weeks.

"Do you think we should get some decorations?" Jason asked as we pushed the cart down very crowded, narrow aisles. He stopped in front of the wall of streamers and banners. "Is blue a good color scheme? Or maybe yellow?"

"These are for baby showers," I answered, staring at a banner of woodland animals cheering *It's a Boy!* Next to it were a group of sea creatures shouting *It's a Girl!* I briefly wondered which group would win in a fight. Street rules preferably.

"So no?" Jason asked. He glanced quickly at the woodland creatures. "I feel like they don't fit the vibe of the party I'm trying to plan."

"The baby shower banners don't fit the vibe of the party you're trying to plan?" I asked. "I mean, I prefer the sea creatures over the woodland animals."

"What about this?" Jason picked up a rainbow banner that declared *You're 40!*

"None of us are *that* old," I said.

"Yeah, but we can mix the letters around and make our own signs," Jason said. His eyes lit up. "Yes! We'll do that!"

And so we filled the cart with baby shower, birthday, retirement, and any other celebration banner we could find. Jason also insisted on buying plastic champagne flutes instead of using red solo cups. He also bought *tons* of tissue paper. I mean, tons of it. It took up most of the cart.

"What are you doing with these?" I asked.

"I am going to make tissue paper decorations," he said. "I saw it online."

"But what kind?" I asked.

"I'll figure it out later," Jason said.

We pushed the cart in silence for a bit. "I think the tissue paper is bad for the environment," I said. "You know, because you can't recycle it. And Ana would be upset if she saw all that waste - she's the president of the Environmental Club, remember?"

Jason's eyes widened. "Shit! I forgot!" he said. He spun the cart around and started to put back the tissue paper. It took some time. Since the cart was filled with it.

"Don't tell her I considered buying it, okay?" Jason asked as he scurried to return the tissue paper that would most definitely be the end of trees everywhere.

"Ugh, why?" I asked. "Because you still got a thing for her?"

Jason's face reddened as he finished placing the last of the tissue paper back on its shelf. "Whatever, Ains," he grumbled.

"Ew! You do have a thing for her!" I shouted.

"Shhhh," Jason snapped, glancing around nervously.

"No one cares," I said. I nodded to an older woman browsing the greeting cards. She nodded back sagely, returning a silent understanding of the complication of having your sibling thirsting after your roommate.

"Don't tell her," he said hastily. "I don't want to

come off as a creep."

"You aren't a creep," I said. "You just get really nervous around her. Which is weird because-" Immediately, I realized my mistake and stopped talking.

"Why is it weird?" Jason asked. He turned from the bags of chips he was now throwing into the cart with the previous fervor of collecting tissue paper. "Why is it weird?" he asked again, shaking the bags of chips at me. He looked like a very confused squirrel who wasn't sure if these chips were the right choices to hoard for winter.

"It's fine," I said, pretending to be interested in the beef jerky hanging on an endcap.

"Ains," Jason said. He sounded so desperate. "Does she like me? Did she say something?"

"Ugh, *fine*," I said. "Yes, she does like you too. This is so high school." At the look of Jason's face, I added, "And don't tell her I told you. She'd kill me. She's weird about you too."

"Okay," Jason said. "Okay. So this party has to be amazing."

I eyed the contents of the cart. "Something like that."

With a renewed interest in his TRD legacy, Jason began working his way through the grocery aisle with the intensity of a connoisseur. "It's important to choose the snacks before I pick up the bags," Jason explained to me.

I stopped in my tracks. "The bags of what?" There were so many chips already in the cart.

"Uh, wine, stupid," he shot back. "Remember it's a *wine and cheese* party."

"Don't mansplain wine and cheese parties to me," I snapped. "You're buying *bags* of wine for this thing?"

"Yeah," Jason said. "Unless ticket sales do well."

My head was beginning to hurt. "What ticket sales?"

Jason looked confused. "Ticket sales to the wine and cheese. What is wrong with you today?"

"What's wrong with *me*?" I asked. "You're the one not making any sense! What the hell are you talking about?"

Jason sighed and looked up from his very difficult decision making between the three choices of chips available. "We don't have any real budget," he said. "So E.K. had the idea of selling tickets to the party.

We're going to offer an *experience* rather than just a wine and cheese party."

"A wine and cheese experience?" I repeated. "What would that entail?"

"I'm not sure," Jason admitted. "I'm thinking we have some live music and/or a performance after the cocktail hour."

"There's going to be a cocktail hour?" I asked. "Before the wine?"

"No, it's the wine," Jason answered.

"Wines aren't cocktails!"

"It's an expression, Ains!"

"Okay, okay," I said. I was becoming too involved, especially when we all knew how this was going to end. "What kind of live music? Also, what performance?"

"Um, *Who's Afraid of Virginia Woolf?*" Jason said, although it sounded like he was making a guess.

"You and your fraternity brothers are going to perform *Who's Afraid of Virginia Woolf?* for all of your guests at the wine and cheese party, where wine is both wine and cocktail?"

"You sound so negative right now, Ains," Jason huffed as he resumed his chip consideration. A moment later, he looked back at me. "Also, be sure to buy a ticket when we start advertising."

"I don't even get a free ticket!" I cried. "I'm bringing my roommates! Including Ana!"

"Ugh, gross," Jason said. "Ana is her own person and not some property. She is coming with you, but you are not bringing her as one would bring wine to a party."

"You mean a bag of wine," I grumbled.

Suddenly, Jason spotted something from across the dollar store. "YES!" he shouted, startling my new friend who had left greeting cards and was also perusing the snack aisle. He sprinted toward it, as though he was terrified someone would swoop in and grab the small garbage bucket, suitable for a bathroom. He held it triumphantly to his chest, grinning at me. "This," he said, gesturing to the garbage can emphatically, "is *exactly* what we need."

A week later, the Frisbees arrived. After Jason and his brothers brainstormed the best way to sell tickets, they went back to the dollar store and bought twenty-five Frisbees. Using a black marker, they wrote across it: "TRD Wine & Cheese! $23! Friday!"

Unfortunately, since they wrote the first part so

big, the rest of the information - the price and the actual day of the party - was too small so you weren't sure what was flying at you except for the giant letters that spelled out "TRD." They had made flying TRDs.

Now that the weather was nice, everyone was hanging outside. Jason and his brothers would chuck the Frisbees at groups of people, who would then look curiously at the writing. Suddenly, one of them would appear and with their Venmo at the ready, try to convince people to purchase tickets to the party. This worked about 15% of the time.

Another unfortunate: it rained for two days that week, so by Thursday, Frisbees were being chucked at unsuspecting people with a frenzy that resembled flying saucers confusedly floating too close to the ground. Also, at this point, the twenty-five had diminished to thirteen because some dogs and other students ran off with them at the beginning of the week.

Padma, Ana, and I sat on a nearby bench sipping our boba and watching whatever this was.

"You have to admit," Padma said, "they are truly dedicated to this party."

"Experience," I corrected. "There's going to be a

live performance."

"Of what?" Ana asked.

"Music or Virgina Woolf," I said.

"Well, I'm excited to go," Padma said. "Party or experience, I feel like we could all use a break."

"It has been a challenging semester," I said. "With everything going on."

Ana sighed dramatically. "Please don't start with this, Ains," she said. "We can't have another Mal conversation."

"What are you talking about?" I said. "I haven't seen either of you all week!"

"I think Ana just means we're having a nice time," Padma said in her soothing, please-stop-arguing voice. "And you didn't need to bring up Mal."

"Um, I didn't," I said. "Ana did."

"Here we go again," Ana said.

"Okay, just forget it," I said hastily. "I don't want to fight."

"Good, neither do we," Ana said.

"Other news!" Padma said, trying to deflect. "Should we bring anything to this party?"

"No, they'll have the cheese and the bags of wine," I said. "We just need to get tickets."

"We didn't get them yet?!" Ana shouted. "What if they run out?" She looked panicked as a TRD sailed smoothly past us.

I watched as a few people started shouting at Jason and E.K. when a Frisbee landed a bit too close to a group. "It should be fine," I said.

"Seventy-two dollars (there was an additional fee for not buying "early bird" on Monday. My brother is the worst), an outfit change, and a Lyft later in the evening, we were standing on the doorstep of the TRD house.

"This is going to be so much fun!" Ana said. She looked nervous. "Do you think Jason is there yet?"

"You mean at the house where he lives?" I said. "Yes, I'm sure."

Padma rang the doorbell. Or tried to. It didn't work. She banged her fist on the door.

Very similar to a haunted house, the door slowly opened. No one was there, but we heard sounds coming from the kitchen. Linking our arms together, my roommates and I prepared ourselves for a wine and cheese experience.

The Wine and Cheese Experience

Sometimes college parties provide a necessary escape from the long, stressful days of studying and worrying about the future. They also provide an important opportunity for socialization that often gets lost during a week filled with assignments, classes, study labs…and worrying about the future. Jason's "wine and cheese experience" was meant to be that college party that did all of the above, but also would provide core memories that will stick with his guests long into their middle age, where they will reminisce and wax poetic about their college years. This party (ahem, *experience*) will definitely be a cornerstone of treasured college memories. Just not for the reasons Jason hoped for.

The party (ahem, *experience*) itself was the worst thing Ains, Padma, and Ana had ever been to. Actually, it was the worst party anyone had ever been to. And that is saying something because Tim, who agreed to go on a whim when the Frisbee hit the back of his head, got diarrhea at his ninth birthday party right before it was time to open presents. This party (ahem, *experience*) was worse than missing out on opening presents due to explosive and painful diarrhea.

It wasn't so much that it was in a frat house off-campus, but more so that it was a frat house designed to look like what they believed was a high-end, luxury experience. Aside from the one lawn chair in the corner facing the wall as though it was being punished for its existence and, through no fault of its own, was missing its seat, there weren't many places to sit. This may have been due to the fact that the room had to serve multiple purposes - the table with the wine and cheese spread, a dance floor, and a small, modest beer pong table. Ains noticed the beer pong table and wondered, rather mockingly, if it would get moved during the live performance (it did not, adding to the guests' discomfort).

The three of them stood in the doorway, surveying the scene. It was still early, so there was still time to witness firsthand whatever this was supposed to be. Jason smiled widely and waved an arm around, knocking over a stack of organic chemistry books. "Make yourself at home," he declared. He had dressed for the occasion, wearing his best polo shirt, and felt a good host - *social chair*, if you will - should be on hand to greet his guests, even if one of those guests was his awful sibling who didn't believe in what he was trying to achieve.

Ains glared at him, opened their mouth to speak, but then thought better of it. Ains probably thought "no thank you" would have been discouraging, and so decided to say nothing at all. (Jason felt his sibling was a bit less awful at that moment.)

"Seriously," Jason said grandly, with the air of that aviator guy (was it Leonardo DiCaprio?) or the air of that guy Gatsby (that was *definitely* Leonardo DiCaprio). "Come on in. We're happy to have you here." As he turned with a flourish, raising an imaginary glass, Jason knocked over another stack of organic chemistry books.

Ains, Padma, and Ana nodded in response and in one motion, similar to a school of glittery fish coated in cucumber melon body spray, moved closer to the depressed lawn chair. "I want to leave," Ains said for what will be the first of many times.

"We are not leaving," Ana snapped. "We paid for these tickets and we're staying. We never get to do anything like this."

Ains sighed, knowing what will follow will be whining about how boring they were and how they need to put themselves out there. But Ains didn't want to be out there. Ains wanted to be home watching a baking show marathon, reading their books, and avoiding eye contact with everyone who felt a good Saturday night was next to a lawn chair missing its own ass.

Seeing the internal struggle, Ana said pointedly, "Think of the trees."

Dammit. She had a point.

"Where are the rest of the guests?" Padma asked. Her eyes darted around the room, trying to figure out which streaming service would make the true crime documentary of their murders. Padma's mom energy was no match for her bloodlust while watching true crime content (her hobby was binging this content and judging those she felt were "too stupid to see it coming). However, now that they were on the precipice of their own possible true crime special, Padma was disappointed to discover that they would also be judged as the stupid people who didn't see it coming. For $23 a ticket, Padma and her roommates were going to be featured in a true crime documentary. Probably on Tubi because the bigger streaming services felt this was too easy of a murder. "Tickets were how much?" People would post online during their hate watches. "And they bought them?

For a wine and cheese party at a *frat house?*"

Jason looked around the room as though finally noticing that no one had showed up. "Fuck, man," he said to Padma. "I don't actually know." He turned toward the kitchen. "Hey, Trash Bag!" he called.

A lumbering form appeared in the doorway. "Yeah?" He glanced at the three roommates, at Jason, and at the lawn chair.

"Where's the party, man?" Jason asked him.

"The party?" Trash Bag repeated. He also glanced around the mostly empty room.

At this point, Padma's terror was starting to become contagious. Ains and Ana stared at each other in disbelief and they looked to Padma for confirmation. "What. Is. Happening," Ains said through clenched teeth.

"Maybe we're really early," Padma suggested, trying to keep her voice light.

One of the victims, she heard the narrator of their Tubi documentary say, *was the dumbest of the three as she maintained a very positive, almost ridiculous, attitude until the very end.*

Trash Bag didn't wait for a response to his question. Instead he went back into the kitchen. Jason shrugged and gave us a small smile. "I'm thinking we didn't sell as many tickets as we wanted to," he confessed. "No one believed it was a real wine and cheese party." Catching himself, he self-corrected, "I mean, a wine and cheese *experience.*"

Ains was tempted to ask what a real wine and cheese experience meant, but memories of their dollar store shopping trip were still fresh. "But you threw all those Frisbees," Ains said, choosing mockery instead of an informative tone.

Before Jason could offer a nasty retort in response, another group walked through the door. It was three women and two men, who first looked around in confusion as they took in the group already there and the setup of the room. Jason noted that they were obviously better guests because they then excitedly descended upon the cheese table and began to fill their plates.

Ains smirked with their usual, "I told you so," face and turned to Jason. "This is a great party."

Not catching their mocking tone, Jason beamed. This night was already off to a great start. Now he can impress Ana with all of his wine and cheese knowledge from his full forty minutes of online research. Turning to Ana, he said, "Let me show you the cheeses." He offered his arm in a way that would make Jane Austen proud and escorted Ana to the table.

One down. Two to go. Padma and Ains looked at each other. "I'm going to get some wine," Padma said, wandering off to the kitchen.

Ains dejectedly stayed behind. *I guess it's just you and me, lawn chair.*

*****

Despite the nonexistent slow start at the beginning, the party (ahem, *experience*) did pick up an hour later and people were starting to enjoy themselves. Well, most people.

For starters, Jason and Ana were playing a very awkward game of "will-they-won't-they" with a heavy emphasis on "what is actually happening here." One minute Jason was trying to get Ana's attention and the next she was trying to get his attention. They were so concerned with getting the other to notice them that it looked as though they were having two different conversations across the room. Jason would say something over his shoulder that Ana couldn't hear, then turn around to find Ana gone. Meanwhile, Ana was in a separate area of the room talking to an imaginary Jason. They have yet to figure out this method of confusing coquettishness was preventing either of them from having a normal interaction within hearing distance for the rest of the night.

"So I discovered that most wine and cheese parties begin with the host introducing the cheese," Jason explained to what he thought was Ana next to him. "But I didn't discover that until twenty minutes before the party (ahem, *experience*) started, so we made these little signs."

"My week went really well," Ana said to what she thought was Jason next to her. "But I'm really excited to be here. I don't know much about wine or cheese, so I'm looking forward to reading these little signs."

"How did your week go?" Jason asked the cluster of houseplants to his left. "I've been so busy planning this. Did Ains tell you all of the great stuff we got at the dollar store?"

"How did you pick the bags of wine?" Ana asked the earlier stack of organic chemistry books. "Did you find this menu online?"

And so this conversation continued with both parties nervously looking anywhere but each other. However, they did manage to dazzle all of the inanimate objects with their respective wit and personalities in a way that would make Belle very jealous in her own enchanted castle.

It's a shame that Jason and Ana didn't make eye contact because they would have had a lot to discuss regarding the choice in décor. Using the mix and match finds from the dollar store, the TRD housemates created a series of signs using the letters from the different banners. With a mix of letter sizes, colors, and themes, the banners overhead resembled the most cheerful ransom notes:

CoMe **THI**s W**Y**

join THE parTy

WELCOME, **BABY**!

RETIRE to WARMING HOUSE

HAPPY PARTY!

LET'S dRiNK happy DAY

Oh YES! RETirE heRE

As a college student herself, Padma understood the importance of being thrifty. But there was thrifty and there was a terrifying mix of misspellings and misuse of syntax. Despite the backdrop of woodland animals and sea creatures, the scenes felt threatening. But who or what they were threatening, or why, still remained to be seen. She stared at the banners sprinkled around the room with the sudden realization that she was completely alone yet surrounded by incoming guests and the unhinged TRDs who put together these signs.

The narrator's voice returned: *It should have been a fun Friday night with friends, but instead turned into a sinister start to the weekend. As the lowest members of the social hierarchy, this group of TRDs may have been planning something that would ensure everyone knew their names.*

CUT TO: Stock images of college students that seem almost cultish (but with the right lighting and budget from a good streaming service would get the point across). Then, a picture of Padma appears on the screen, smiling as she holds her books in front of her.

Narrator: *Padma, one third of the Roommate Trio [this is the title that Padma is thinking of for the documentary, but is still workshopping this], first noticed something amiss with the broken lawn chair. A sign for sure that the bottom will drop out [pause for dramatic effect and macabre humor], she chose to stay and came face-to-face with decorations that served as Oracles to her demise.*

Despite the horrific decor, Padma smiled, quite pleased with herself. Maybe she had a future as a true crime documentarian.

"It's interesting that people would consider cheddar to be the most popular cheese, but I am partial to the softer cheese," said someone at Padma's elbow, making her jump out of her reverie. It was a shame because Padma was just about to accept her True Crime Award for On Screen: Outstanding Two-Part Docuseries (it's important to note here that Padma had decided, in a matter of seconds, that she would survive whatever true crime situation awaited them so she would have full creative control over her life story. It would really suck if someone else got the credit and all she got was this shitty wine and cheese party. Sorry, *experience*). "Oh sorry," the voice at the elbow said. Then: "Wait a minute…"

"Ana?" Padma said. "Weren't you talking to Jason?"

"I was!" Ana said. "I thought you were him."

"No," Padma gestured across the room where Jason was laughing with the houseplants. "He's all the way over there." Then: "Were you talking about cheese this *entire time*?"

Ana's face reddened. "I did forty minutes of online research! I came prepared with talking points!"

"Well, then, I guess go get 'em?" Padma said with uncertainty. She pushed Ana gently in the direction of the Plant Whisperer. Then she turned around to look for Ains. She didn't have far to go.

Ains had made their way over to the cheese table and Padma noticed the horror, betrayal, and rage competing for space in their facial expression. She hurried over.

For Ains, the biggest disappointment of the evening was the cheese.

The cheese was not good.

Billed as the pièce de résistance of the wine

and cheese party (ahem, *experience*), the cheese felt more proverbial. The wine did too since no wine was actually purchased for this evening. As it was explained to Ains in agonizing detail punctuated with many pauses by Trash Bag, Team TRD ran over budget very quickly, resulting in cheap beer and wine coolers made into popsicle sticks, which were now melting on the kitchen counter.

"Someone did have the innovation to place the frozen abominations into paper cups," Ains explained sadly to Padma.

"Are they any good?" Padma asked.

"It's like the saddest metaphor for our childhood," Ains continued.

"I can tell you're upset because a simile uses 'like' or 'as' and you should know better," Padma said, staring at the cups with the popsicle sticks poking out.

"It's a metaphor for childhood," Ains tried again. "A childhood looking at us all in the rearview mirror. Can't you see the smiling group of children waving enthusiastically as we drive to our new home in Adult World?"

Padma's eyes widened. "OMG, I can," she said, realizing Ains needs to survive the night too so she could get the writing credit.

Now that there was an audience, Ains went into Full English Major Mode. "There they are, Padma, talking amongst themselves of the great adventures we would have in our new home. I can't bear to tell those hypothetical adolescents what lies beyond that corner is bad music, uncomfortable social situations, and these wine-sicles turning into a sad puddle of synthetic colors in a bright red cup."

"Uh-huh," said Padma, regretting giving Ains the head writer job in her head. This was a bit too maudlin. She didn't want to bum anyone out with her On Screen: Outstanding Two-Part Docuseries.

Bad drinks and melodrama aside, the true betrayal should lie within the cheese. The cheese was not good.

Dearest Reader, perhaps you did not read this properly. The. Cheese. Was. Not. Good.

This "cheese" sat on a six foot long folding table with bits of dirt from whatever ungodly use it had before. Placed throughout the table were different color paper plates - white paper plates that someone colored in with magic markers around the edges. The marker edges were squiggles and misshapen pictures that could be hearts, or testicles - both would feel at home in this space. Next to these cheese plates were jaunty signs labeled "Cheddar!" "Good-A!" "American!" "French!" "This One!" also decorated with the same confusing shapes and squiggles. There were twelve different plates, but seven of these plates, despite their cheerful messages, were just American Cheese singles.

As Padma and Ains contemplated what events led them to this moment surrounded by luke-warm cheese and no bags of wine, Ana and Jason finally found each other and were engaging in some sort of conversation with each other:

"Your hair smells really good," Jason said to Ana.

"Thanks," Ana said. "It's hairspray."

"I like the hairspray you chose," Jason said.

But before Jason and Ana could list hairsprays that they both liked, Ains had tracked them down with Padma in tow. "You owe me $23," Ains said. Then, gesturing around the room at the other twenty-two people there - almost one for each Frisbee - said, "You owe all of us $23. Each."

"Why?" Jason asked, confused. This party (ahem, *experience*) was exactly what he planned, from the decorations down to the cheese table.

Not attempting to hide their rage, Ains gestured to the table and its sweaty pile of cheese liars. "For whatever this is supposed to be," Ains said.

Jason shook his head. "No way," he said. "You're getting your money's worth."

"Where, Jason? Where do you see my $23? Or anyone's $23 dollars?"

Jason smiled and waved his arm around, knocking over a pile of economics textbooks. "It's in the memories," he said sagely. "We're making memories."

"Jason, I am going to murder you in your sleep," Ains said through gritted teeth. Padma made a face because two different murders in one special bordered on melodramatic (*We'll cut this moment from the recreated scene, she decided*). Of course, Jason didn't hear his sibling's not-very-veiled threat because he had moved on to share his clever response with Ana. He got through half the story before he discovered she was not standing next to the potted plant but was, in fact, speaking to the potted plant.

Unfortunately, love will have to wait because the live music portion needed to begin. He excused himself with Ana (she didn't hear, but the plant did) and rushed off to find Electric Kettle. E.K. was the self-identified artist of the group and had graciously offered to be the live entertainment. "E.K.," Jason hissed. "Are you ready?"

"Col," E.K. said, using the shortened version of Jason's nickname, Colander. "I was born ready." Then he paused. "But I need, like, ten minutes to set up."

"Got it," Jason said. "I'll vamp with the introduction."

Jason wished there was a front of the room or that they thought to install an actual stage during party prep. Instead, his options were the sad lawn chair and the couch with people already sitting on it. He chose the couch because the lawn chair had already been through so much.

"Attention, distinguished guests," Jason said, clapping his hands, realizing too soon that he should have turned the music off. He fumbled for his phone and the music stopped. The silence felt a bit awkward, as everyone looked around in confusion. "Ahem," Jason tried again. "Distinguished guests, may I have your attention please?" Now everyone was looking at him. Oh, crap. "Distinguished guests, the live entertainment portion of the evening will be starting soon. We hope you enjoyed the cocktail hour and I would like to bring out the chef that made tonight's wine and cheese experience possible. Trash Bag? Can you come in here?"

Trash Bag appeared in the doorway, wearing his "Food Bitch" apron. "What can I do for you, my party people?" he said.

Jason gestured grandly to Trash Bag, almost falling off the couch, but certainly knocking over the stack of Victorian literature novels next to it. "Distinguished guests," Jason announced, "Your chef for the evening!"

The crowd - all twenty-two guests (again, SO close to the full Frisbee run!) and nine fraternity brothers - were split in their appreciation of Trash Bag's culinary contribution. About half of the guests clapped politely because they were the ones that had been confused over the cheese table offerings and the distressing lack of wine for what was advertised as a wine and cheese experience. The other half of the guests and the nine fraternity brothers roared their admiration. The lukewarm reception and the white-hot fandom mingled together to create sizzling pockets of excitement, confusion, fatigue, and sycophancy throughout the room. Trash Bag gave a little bow as his fraternity brothers chanted "Food Bitch! Food Bitch! Food Bitch!"

When everyone finally quieted, Issac, who had watched his roommate Tim get hit with the Frisbee that brought them here and had also heard the ninth birthday diarrhea story from Tim's mom, had to ask: "Who's the Food Bitch? You or the person reading it?"

The room hushed. Trash Bag surveyed the room, stopping briefly on the table full of cheese that had been purchased in haste just 24 hours earlier, and spoke the words that left such a chilling effect on the partygoers that they would repeat this to others well into middle age in an attempt to understand its meaning:

"We're *all* the Food Bitch."

*****

After Trash Bag left everyone unsettled physically (the cheese *had* been sitting out for awhile) and spiritually (who or what constitutes a "Food Bitch" left everyone with their own theories), it was E.K.'s turn to both delight and terrify the guests. Jason had emphatically promised an "experience" and he hoped Electric Kettle, the more responsible of his fraternity brothers, would deliver.

It is unclear if Electric Kettle delivered the live performance Jason or the guests expected, but it was clear that Electric Kettle had only thought of his live performance about an hour before the wine and cheese party (ahem, *experience*) began. E.K. had set up a karaoke machine in the hopes of living out his dream of becoming a rock star. Unfortunately, he borrowed the karaoke machine from his mother and the song database was filled mostly with anthems for the moms who had high hopes in college and are still wondering where their potential went as they pull stress-inducing double duty in both professional and domestic responsibilities. In short, it was mostly Katy Perry, Pat Benatar, and Britney Spears. E.K. wasn't too familiar with any of these songs, so the promised live performance centered on warbled renditions of "you go, girl" anthems.

As polite party guests do, everyone applauded politely at the end of each song, which seemed to take forever. Unfortunately, E.K. misinterpreted the polite clapping for a job well done and began to work the room with each new song. His unwavering eye contact during "Toxic" left everyone feeling a bit queasy. In retrospect, it may have also been the cheese which had now begun to sweat more than E.K. when he realized, too late into the song, that he couldn't hit the high notes in "We Belong."

The party (ahem, *experience*) continued to crawl along, lacking the self-awareness that it needed to be put out of its misery. Jason continued to work the room as the great social chair he believed he could be, but even he was starting to lose steam. The truth was everyone wanted to have fun at this party (ahem, *experience*) - they really did. Despite the high price tag, it was the same group of people, the same music, the same expectations of what they did every Saturday night. Maybe it was the forced frivolity or maybe it was - *dammit, why is E.K. starting another song?* - a skill set in social planning that Jason was just developing, but this experience just wasn't landing.

Now E.K. had found the maudlin hits on his mother's karaoke machine and the vibe was getting very "what if" and "if only." Jason needed to intervene. "Thank you!" he shouted with what he hoped didn't betray his own existential crisis. "Please join me in thanking Electric Kettle and his musical stylings!"

This time the applause felt a bit more robust - most likely because it was over. E.K. took a bow and headed into the kitchen to celebrate with a melted popsicle of watered down alcohol.

Trash Bag appeared at Jason's elbow. "Should I start getting ready for Virgina Woolf?" he asked.

Shit, Jason thought. *I forgot about Virginia Woolf.* "I don't know," Jason said to Trash Bag. "Do you think this is the right crowd?"

Trash Bag considered the room. "Only one way to find out."

By the time the TRDs finished the opening scene of *Who's Afraid of Virginia Woolf?*, most of the party (ahem, *experience*) had cleared out and Jason had his answer.

*****

As a witness to the worst party (ahem, *experience*) ever planned, Ains had moved into the kitchen as soon as Martha ordered George to answer the door.

As much as it included the same people, the same music, and the same expectation for a Saturday night, Ains's problem still remained: something needed to change. There was an itchiness under Ains's skin and the need to keep moving forward, and wherever this need was coming from, it felt unsettling.

"Screw you!" screamed Trash Bag as Martha.

"You're drunk again," retorted Jason as George.

Look, this party (ahem, *experience*) was a disaster. But Ains felt proud of Jason for taking a chance, for trying to do something new. Stirring the popsicle stick weeping into the red solo cup, Ains peeked in at what they hoped was the final attempt at a live performance. Trash Bag was a great Martha with seething resentment toward Jason as the weak, yet formidable opponent, George. E.K. played both parts of the befuddled couple Nick and Honey very well.

As distressing as all of this was to watch, Ains couldn't look away. Of course, Ana loved every second of it, gasping at the right moments and applauding enthusiastically every time Jason delivered a line. Padma had determined, with a little disappointment, that they were all safe from any attempts on their lives. She had crafted an extraordinary On Screen:

Outstanding Two-Part Docuseries out of this evening and to go back to reality, with whatever was happening at the front of the room, felt almost cruel by comparison.

Jason was so wrapped up in his performance that after Trash Bag/Martha finished singing, he noticed that most of the party (ahem, *experience*) had cleared out. The only people left were Ains, Padma, and Ana, each surveying whatever was happening at the front of the room with three different expressions.

Oh, and Tim and Issac. They stayed behind because they had nowhere else to go on a Saturday night. After that ninth birthday party incident, Tim spent most of his young adulthood struggling to make friends.

*****

It took some convincing, but by 11pm, everyone left had convinced Jason that they did have a wonderful "wine and cheese experience," but they needed to salvage what was left of the night. Eventually Jason agreed to throw out the horror show also known as the cheese table and start inviting people to a standard

Saturday night party.

It helped that he was able to break out the dollar store garbage can. Jason had originally conceived it as a punchbowl of sorts, so it helped that he was able to take the leftover beer and wine coolers and combine them all into the small garbage can.

And, yes, that sounds just as disgusting as you think it is.

"Can we go *now*?" Ains asked as Jason and Ana happily combined alcohol that should never mix, even in the stomachs of young people.

"Why do you want to leave?" Padma asked. "The party's just getting started."

"All of the previous attempts at fine culture left me tired," Ains said drily.

"Ains, you need to get out more," Padma said. "This night actually turned out okay."

"I guess," Ains said.

Padma looked over at her friend. "Are you okay?" Padma asked. "This isn't about Mal, is it?"

At that Ains bristled. "No!" Ains retorted. "Just stop, okay? Maybe I'm just feeling a little lost lately. And before you can ask me again, no, this has nothing to do with Mal. But it seems that you and Ana would love it if I was still a mess over it."

Padma rolled her eyes. "Actually, we would love it if we could move on."

"But I have moved on!" Ains shouted, not caring that Tim and Issac were looking over curiously. "It's everyone else that wants me to stay the same!"

Padma studied Ains curiously. Something *had* been up lately. A while back, Ains had come back from class late and gave no indication of where they were other than they were at the Student Center. But Ains had seemed in good spirits, so Padma didn't ask any more questions. It was Ana that suggested that maybe Ains had started seeing Mal again and wanted to keep it from the two of them. Now Padma wasn't sure who to believe.

"I just want you to be happy," Padma said, wincing at how that sounded. She didn't mean it, but it came out in a patronizing tone. "I mean, we both want you to be happy."

"Why were you talking to Mal that day?" Ains demanded suddenly.

Padma sighed. "I thought you said it wasn't about Mal," she said.

"It isn't, but now I'm suddenly curious."

"You've been drinking."

"So have you."

"Ains, I can't do this right now, okay?"

"Just answer the question, Padma. Please. That's all I'm asking. What did you and Mal talk about?"

Padma was quiet for a moment. She looked at the scene in the kitchen, everyone busy with their roles, happy to do what was asked of them. And here she was, with this shitty job of having to tell Ains the truth. Of course, Ana was no help at the moment. Better to get it over with.

Turning to Ains, Padma sighed and told her the truth: "I wasn't talking to Mal about you. Mal is a piece of shit. I caught Mal cheating on you and that day, they confessed that they had been seeing someone for awhile. I told Mal *I* was going to tell you if they didn't break up with you. Then Mal dragged their feet like a fucking coward and now you're going to blame me because I was put in an impossible situation. Mal is selfish and you didn't deserve that. But I also didn't want to get between the two of you. And, yes, we probably shouldn't have let everything try to go back to normal, but I just wanted *one fucking day* without having to take care of someone else." Padma had blurted everything out, but instead of relief, the pit that had been in her stomach since the day it happened only felt heavier.

Ains stared at Padma for what felt like an eternity. Then Ains turned and left the room. *Great*, Padma thought. *Just great.*

Jason looked over at that moment. "You good?"

"Yeah, I guess," Padma said. "Yeah, it's all good."

"Good," Jason said. He offered the garbage can to Padma. "Want to have the first sip?"

Padma stared at the contents. It seemed impossible to commit another crime against wine, but here it was. "Absolutely fucking not."

*****

Ains wasn't mad at Padma - not really. It was a combination of embarrassment, confusion, relief to finally know, and maybe a *bit* of anger mixed in. All of Ains's emotions roiled, creating a disgusting cocktail that would rival whatever was in that garbage can/ punchbowl.

Which is why Ana found Ains helping Trash Bag with his persuasive essay (due tomorrow at midnight) rather than being back at the party (ahem, *experience*). After Ains had walked out, Padma had pulled Ana aside and explained what happened.

"What?" Ana exclaimed. "Why would you tell Ains what happened?"

"Because I didn't want to keep it a secret from our best friend!" Padma answered. "I felt bad enough."

Ana sighed. "Now it's going to be a thing."

"No, it's not," Padma said. "Ains just needs time to process."

Ana rolled her eyes and set off to find Ains. And there they were, explaining to Trash Bag how to make the in-text citations fit the margins. As wordsmiths go, Trash Bag had a strong handle on his ideas; it was really the verbal portion of his personality that left the audience wanting.

"What are you doing?" Ana hissed, pulling Ains away from Trash Biag and his essay.

"Trash Bag needs to finish this or he's going to fail for the semester," Ains answered. "He didn't have time before because he was working on the cheese spread for tonight."

Ana's face turned pink, a sure sign to Ains that she was getting angrier. "Why can't you at least *try* to have fun?"

Ains shrugged. "I tried. It's just not my scene." This wasn't true, but it felt like a powerful thing to say. Something that would cause a reaction. Ains was right.

"Oh, it isn't?" Ana said. "I see. I didn't know you were above all of this."

"I don't mean that," Ains protested, glancing around the room. "It's just all ridiculous, isn't it?"

"Ridiculous?" Ana's face had reached full magenta at this point.

"Well, yeah." Ains gave a half laugh. "They don't even have real cheese."

"Um, yes we do," Trash Bag volunteered from his desk chair. "And we labeled it."

"You're right," Ana said. "Great work, Trash Bag." To Ains, Ana said, "Did you think that maybe everyone is trying their best?"

"No, not really," Ains answered. Again, Ains didn't mean to say this, but the itchiness under their skin was getting worse. And so it was another direct hit.

"Look," Ana said. "I get it - you're feeling shitty about everything that happened with Mal. But it doesn't make it okay for you to make other people feel shitty. If you want to leave, you can leave. It's not the best night or the best wine or the best cheese or any wine and cheese, but we're all here and that's what I care about the most."

"I'm sorry," Ains began. "I just don't see the point to all of this."

Ana sighed and closed her eyes for a moment. "I'm sorry you don't see it either." She turned and left the room.

From his desk chair, Trash Bag cleared his throat. "I know you're, like, dealing with stuff, but I have a question about my thesis statement."

Ains sighed and looked over Trash Bag's shoulder. "Okay, so here you need to address the *how* and the *why* rather than just the *why*."

"Is it worth it?" Trash Bag asked, eyes on his screen, typing away.

"Well, it's part of the rubric, so I guess?"

"I don't mean the essay. I mean the rubric of *life*," Trash Bag said. "Is it worth it to fight with your roommates?"

"I don't want to fight with them!" Ains said. "I'm just confused right now."

"Ya'll need to work this out," Trash Bag said. "Roommate relationships are the most sacred. Look at Jason. This party was the *worst*."

Ains blinked in surprise. "But you helped."

"Of course, we're going to help our brother! Colander does so much for us. But he's also really fussy and gets these weird ideas that we need to be cultured or whatever. I don't want to be cultured. I want to get a couple of kegs and some snacks and do a marathon-watch of Star Wars."

"Even *Rogue One?*" Ains asked.

"Especially *Rogue One!*" Trash Bag said. "But Jason wanted to do this *experience* crap and we wanted to be there for him. Because roommates help each other."

"Then why didn't Padma help me?" Ains asked.

"Cause that shit is complicated," Trash Bag said. "And you know it. If Padma told you, you would be pissed at her for telling you, right?"

"And if she didn't, I would still be pissed that she kept it from me," Ains finished, sighing heavily. "I get it."

"But Padma, who hates confrontation, told Mal what was up and Mal *still* fucked up," Trash Bag finished. "So it sounds like Padma did her best. Wait, is this a journal article?"

"Yeah," Ains said. "You cite the author. So what do you suggest?"

"I don't know," Trash Bag said. "But I know that I wouldn't keep fighting with my roommates. I'm graduating this semester and that shit sucks knowing we won't be able to get into petty drama after this."

Ains was quiet for a moment. "Thanks, Lucas."

"Don't worry about it, champ," Lucas said, trying to get used to the fact that in the real world, grown-ups aren't called Trash Bag by their peers.

Once Ains felt confident that Lucas had a handle on his paper, they decided to head back to the party (ahem, *experience*). As Ains was leaving, an embroidered pillow on the bed caught their eye: Everything happens for a reason. *What the fuck?* Ains thought, leaving the room, all confusion over Food Bitch forgotten as this pillow entered Ains's consciousness.

*****

Poor Jason. His night of culture fell apart the minute it turned into a normal college party (ahem, *experience*). Between the loud music, a crowd around the beer pong table, and people starting to wreck the place, he felt defeated.

Ains appeared at his side, "You okay, big brother?"

Jason looked at his sibling before surveying the typical scene unfolding. "Yeah, I guess. I just wanted something different tonight, you know?"

"It was different," Ains said. "I can honestly tell you it was definitely not what we expected for this evening."

Jason eyed Ains warily, but his little sibling met his eye without any mockery. It was all genuine. "I'm proud of you," Ains continued. "You tried something new. It didn't quite work, but you tried it."

"It didn't?" Jason said.

"Come on," Ains said, laughing. "If E.K. didn't bum everyone out, you and Trash Bag's rendition of an unhappy married couple definitely did."

Jason laughed. "Okay, maybe you're right. We should have practiced more. We just have so much chemistry, you lmow?"

"Yeah, that's what it was," Ains replied. The two stood in silence as someone knocked over the pathetic lawn chair, stumbled for a bit, and then landed ass-first into the wall, leaving behind a giant butt print. "Did you know about that pillow in Trash Bag's room?" Ains asked suddenly.

"'Everything happens for a reason?'" Jason replied. "Yeah, he got that at a Joann's sale one day. He said he needed the energy boost."

"Huh, it's a good one," Ains said.

Ana and Padma appeared next to them. "Everyone okay?" Padma asked worriedly.

"Yeah," Ains said. "Everyone's okay." Ains put an arm around Padma in a half hug. Then turned to Ana, "You okay?"

Ana sighed. "Yeah, I'm okay. Sorry about before."

"Sorry about it all."

"Sorry about Mal."

"Fuck Mal."

"Yeah."

The four of them stood in silence, for once enjoying the moment. As they watched the second ass-print of the night appear on the opposite wall, Jason realized he had had enough. "Anyone hungry?"

"Yes," came the chorus of voices.

"I already called an Uber," said a voice behind

them. Paper finished, Trash Bag was gesturing for the door. "Let's get out of here, party people."

"Wow, thanks, Trash Bag," Padma said.

"It's Lucas, by the way," he said.

"Thanks, Lucas," Padma said.

"Really?" Jason said to Lucas.

"Might as well," Lucas said. "It'll all be over soon."

"True," Jason agreed.

Another scream came from the beer pong tournament. Whether it was in defeat or triumph, they didn't stick around to find out. A booth at the diner was waiting for them and they needed another set of core memories before it was too late.

- The Beginning -

"*So we beat on, boats against the current, borne back ceaselessly into the past.*"

- Leonardo DiCaprio

Finals week came and went, as it always does. I packed up my room and found lots of different half-eaten food and crumbs, as I always do. I passed my classes, as I hope to continue to do in my time here. The sun was warming up our dorm room, reminding us that summer was just beginning.

Ana was taking a study abroad course over the summer as part of the immersion for her language major. Padma had an internship lined up in New York City, and she was looking forward to being on her own instead of responsible for younger siblings. As for me, I was heading back to my summer job at the local grocery store in what I hoped was my last summer there.

"Did we clean everything out?" Ana asked anxiously. This was the fifth time she asked us that.

"Yep," Padma answered. "Just like I told you ten minutes ago."

"I just don't want to get a citation for leaving anything behind," Ana said. "It will work against us in the fall. We can't screw up - not after finally getting a spot at The Townhouses."

The Townhouses were the only decent dorm option on campus - slightly off-campus, but still fitting on campus in terms of financial aid and scholarships necessary for paying room and board. A group of roommates got an entire floor of a townhouse to themselves - four rooms on one floor, giving us privacy, yet a communal living space, on the days our roommate codependency got the best of us. The three of us had worked hard to get a spot, including finding a fourth person to live with us. It was a masterclass in relationship building - one that started with Padma making first contact in the "Politics and Sexuality" class that they both shared. *I saw that there was a partner project this semester - do you want to pair up? It would be so great to work with someone who knows what they're doing!*

Ana followed it up by making sure she was at the gym the same time as this new person - that's so crazy that you're here this time too! *Oh, you're heading to your "Politics and Sexuality" class after this? My roommate's in that class too!*

I closed the deal by making sure every flyer they needed approved for their literary magazine was stamped during my student worker shift. *No waiting for my friends! Don't be silly! You don't owe me one - well, if you insist! Wait, really? You know both of my roommates?!*

What's that, dear reader? You don't remember

any of this happening over the course of this book? That's so strange - I'm sure I mentioned it somewhere.

I didn't? Well, I was a bit *busy*, remember?

ANYWAY, now that we had a fourth member, our application was approved and next fall, we will be Townhouse living!

"Hey, after we drop this stuff off in our cars, let's go look at our building," I suggested. It will be months before we move in, but we have already started calling it "our building" and "our rooms."

"Yes!" Ana said. Fortified with a new beginning, we finished cleaning out this old, stupid dorm room that no one cared about anymore. Soon we were on our way across campus to The Townhouses.

"Do you think anyone will let us in?" Padma asked on the way. "I would love to start measuring my single room."

"What color scheme are you all going to use?" I asked, weaving past students and some parents hurrying to finish up and beat traffic.

"Hmmm," Ana said. "I haven't decided yet. Maybe blue because it's relaxing? Or maybe yellow because it's creative?"

"How about we each pick one so we can have

three rooms with different purposes?" I suggested.

"Yes!" Padma exclaimed. "A blue room for relaxing, a yellow room for creativity, and, um, another that -"

"We'll figure it out," I said. "We have all summer."

"That's true - we can make plans to plan out the rooms!" Ana added. Padma and I cheered in agreement.

And there's that Type-A codependency again. Let's hope our new friend dislikes personal boundaries as much as us.

After some squabbling over which number was our Townhouse (#22), we found what we were looking for. The doors were already left open, a sign that everyone was out and waiting for inspection from the Resident Advisors. Taking this as a sign from the dorm gods, we snuck in and checked out our rooms.

As I stood in my own room taking in my 228 square feet of living space for the next year, I saw the wonderful possibilities waiting for me. The beauty of college is the "one more rule" - one more class, one more semester, one more summer, one more exam. The *one more* that will change your future for the better. The *one more* standing in your way to all of these possibilities that life has to offer - you just need to get through that *one more*.

Of course, in my present moment, I didn't know the difference between *one more* and *one last*. All college students are guilty of confusing the two and I was definitely no exception. I didn't know that the *one more* summer at my grocery store job, the one I was heading to next week, would also be the *one last* summer I would be there and see friends I've known for most of my early adulthood. I didn't know that our *one more* semester on campus, starting in the fall, would also be the *one last* time we would all live together before Ana got accepted into a full-year program abroad, Padma would transfer schools to attend an early graduate program, and I would live in a studio apartment alone and off-campus until I moved to New York after graduation. I didn't know that we wouldn't graduate together or spend *one more* summer together going into our final year. I thought *one more* took precedence over *one last*.

Growing up is equal parts lovely and horrible.

The lovely part is the many firsts of adulthood:

- first "real" job
- first independent living space

- first pet that doesn't belong to the entire family
- first time paying your own bills
- first time making friends outside of college

Of course, what we all grow to learn is the horrible part dovetails directly into the lovely high points:

- losing your first "real" job
- having to move from your first independent living space (or even worse, having to move back home to lick your wounds and plan your next move)
- bringing your first pet in to be euthanized after old age and health issues get the best of them
- first time forgetting to pay your own bills and realizing how delicate your economic situation is - one wrong move and everything falls apart
- Losing your close relationship with your college friends - those once-considered permanent landmarks in your personal landscape

If I knew time was so fleeting, I would have stayed in these moments longer. If I had known this time wouldn't last, I would have pulled back on the dramatic outbursts that cost me precious time with my friends. But I didn't know any of this.

That's how stupid college makes you - the bubble of youth is so thickly coated around you, you never consider a time where it may burst. And so, in this moment - in this very cramped single dorm room that kind of smells (just a bit) and needs a cleaning I will never give it - I just listened to the happy squeals of my roommates and the busy sounds of picture taking, room measuring, and question-yelling that was happening on the second floor of Townhouse #22. I didn't know to take it all in and I didn't know to savor any of those moments. I just let all of the present become background noise because I assumed it would be there forever.

Taking a full spin of my room, I didn't noticed the stained carpet (I wouldn't until next October), the cracked ceiling (I wouldn't until the final push of hurricane season in November and I lost $150 in textbooks), and the desk that definitely would not hold my ever-growing book collection (this I noticed the first day of move-in, making the floor my permanent book organizing space which then fell victim to the final push of hurricane season). I just noticed the possibilities because that's college. A delightful combination of stupid and sanguine.

I glanced out my window and noticed Quinn leaving the townhouse across the way. After a few moments of struggling to open a window that was clearly painted shut at some point, I screamed across the courtyard. "Quinn!"

Surprised, Quinn looked up and around, searching for the voice. "I'm here!" I waved, not caring how stupid and Disney-fied this must look.

Quinn's face broke into a smile. "Ains!" they shouted excitedly. "Are we neighbors?"

"Yes, I think so!" I shouted. "Wait, I'll come down to talk."

"Don't worry," Quinn said. "I'll come to you."

Quinn appeared in my doorway fairly quickly and surveyed the space with me. "It looks…exactly like mine."

"Yes," I answered. "The magic of dorm room conformity."

"But it's nice to know that we'll be neighbors," Quinn continued. "Maybe we can hang out more?" The last part trailed off a bit, as though Quinn was unsure of my response. "Lunch was really fun the other day."

"Yes!" I answered again. Only this time, a bit too enthusiastically. *Relax, Ains.* "That would be nice." Again, this last part trailed off a bit, because I was unsure of any response that followed it.

Quinn smiled at me. "Let's plan for a weekly movie night. That way we have something to look forward to."

"Or a weekly book club," I added. "Or a cheese club. Or a weekly…" *What. Is. Happening. Right. Now. Please. Stop. Saying. Words.*

Quinn laughed. "Yes to any of those things. I don't know how much time we will have to read a book a week or how many different types of cheeses that exist -"

Thinking back to the wine and cheese party (ahem, *experience*), I interrupted, "From my experience, not many."

"Well, I think just hanging out with you sounds like a good part of my week," Quinn said.

I studied Quinn for a minute. In my previous dorm room, it would seem strange to have this person I just met be a part of my everyday college life. However, in this new room, in the new semester that awaited me - after the semester I had - I realized that Quinn reminded me that the world is still a big place. And here was someone who didn't find me too much in any way - not too talkative, too dramatic, too strange - and just wanted to be a part of my everyday life. Well, a part of my week. That sounded equal parts easy enough and the most difficult adaptation to consider. But it was a move forward and I knew that's what I needed.

A noise from the doorway made me jump. I look over to see Ana and Padma studying Quinn and me with bemused expressions. "Who's this?" Ana asked.

"This is Quinn," I said. "Quinn, these are two of my roommates, Ana and Padma. We have a third person, but they aren't here yet." Another change: we will now be four roommates. The even number lifted my spirits a bit and I hoped we would have more balance in our friend dynamic.

"Hey," Quinn nodded to them both. "It's really nice to meet you both."

"How do you know Ains?" Padma asked.

"We met during the semester," Quinn answered. "I bumped into Ains at the Student Center."

Ana snorted. "Let me guess - in the middle of a crisis?"

Padma laughed. "Or walking into the glass doors?"

I laughed awkwardly with them. Quinn looked confused. "No, nothing like that. I was at one of the information tables and Ains stopped by. Turns out I'm going to be your neighbor next year."

"Well, you know us now too," Ana said. "So you don't have to worry about just knowing Ains. That won't be too great next semester with just Ains as your neighbor!" Padma laughed with her.

Again, Quinn looked confused. "Yeah, that's great. But Ains-" glancing over at me - "who is very much in the room, is cool to talk to, so I would be fine just knowing Ains in the Townhouses for now."

Padma and Ana looked surprised. They exchanged one of their glances, but it was a new one - a new one! This one seemed to read, *could* we *be the problem too?*

I'm not saying the ground actually shifted, but it

sure as hell felt like something significant happened. Ana and Padma glanced at me with a slight apology in their eyes. Quinn's presence was already shaking up the foundation of our dynamic - many others would do the same in the coming months (spoiler alert: many people, including our fourth roommate). Suddenly, we didn't have to conform to the same roles.

We could be someone else. There was still time.

Maybe the ground did shift because what would happen in the next semester sparked significant changes to *one more* and *one last*. This was the start.

I looked over at Quinn, with a smile on my face. "Don't worry about Ana and Padma, they were just kidding. You'll see - we are definitely a strange group. In a good way." I grinned at my roommates and they seemed to relax. *It's fine*, I told them silently. *We're in this together.*

"Oh really?" Quinn asked, raising an eyebrow. "So I found the weird group to be my neighbors?"

"Oh, sweetie, you have no idea," Padma said. "Be afraid. Be very afraid."

"Just before," Ana added. "Padma was trying to figure out if she wanted to switch rooms with me because of a true crime documentary she saw."

"I don't want to get murdered!" Padma protested.

"But I can?" Ana countered.

"See?" I said to Quinn as they argued over prime murder spots. "We're all mad here."

"Good to know," Quinn said. "Have a week, Ains. I'll text you soon."

"You too," I said. Quinn gave a parting wave to Padma and Ana and headed back outside.

When we heard the door close, my roommates did what they did best - they crowded me with questions and demands to answer. I am happy to say that I had nothing to give them. For once, I wasn't thinking about pairing up or possible relationship pathways. I was just happy to make a new friend.

"Let's just enjoy each other," I said to my roommates. "I'm grateful to have both of you here."

"I agree," Ana said, throwing an arm around each of us. "I am *so* excited for next semester!"

"Let's spend the summer planning the best year ever," Padma suggested. "We are going to take over this place!"

"Yes!" Ana shouted. "And we're all set to go home, so let's stay longer! Lunch?"

"Definitely," Padma said. "I'm not ready to leave

you two yet."

As we headed back outside, each gearing up to fight for our lunch choice, I felt better than I had in a long time. For myself, for my friends, even for the trees. We all made it through another semester with minimal material for our future therapists. This time anyway.

And so we went to lunch, rehashing our semester drama and making promises that felt real in the moment. As we were leaving, my phone buzzed. I looked down.

It's soon, read a text message. *Let me know when you can hang out this summer.* I laughed.

Absolutely, I wrote back. *This weekend?*

I got into my car and started the engine. It felt nice to have things to look forward to.

But that, dear readers, is a story for another day.

About the Author

S. Atzeni (she/they) is a multi-genre, award-winning writer of prose, comics, and academic scholarship. They are the co-author of *The MOTHER Principle* graphic novel series and *The Legend of Dave Bradley* and *W(h)ine and Cheese* in the One 'n Done series. S. Atzeni holds a B.A. in Professional Writing and Journalism and a Master of Arts in English from The College of New Jersey.

S. Atzeni is also the co-founder of Read Furiously Publishing and serves as its Editorial Director and its head of acquisitions, including serving as co-editor of the bestselling *Life in the Garden State* NJ anthology series. Through Read Furiously, S. Atzeni is proud to publish great books, be a part of an amazing independent literary community, and participate in literary activism. S. Atzeni was recently named as part of the "40 under Forty in Publishing" by BookCamp magazine.

A Note to our Furious Readers

From all of us at Read Furiously, we hope you enjoyed our latest installment in our One 'n Done series, *W(h)ine and Cheese.*

Reading is more than a passive activity – it is the opportunity to play an active role to make our world better. We pledge to donate a portion of these book sales to causes that are special to Read Furiously. These causes are chosen with the intent to better the lives of others who are struggling to tell their own stories.

The causes we support encourage a sense of civic responsibility associated with the act of reading. Each cause has been researched thoroughly, discussed openly, and voted upon carefully by our team of Read Furiously editors.

To find out more about who, what, why, and where Read Furiously lends its support, please visit our website at readfuriously.com/our-causes

Happy reading and giving, Furious Readers!

Read Often, Read Well,
Read Furiously!

More in the One 'n Done Series

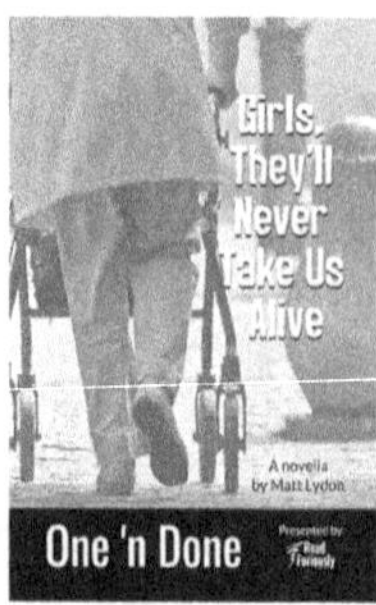

What About Tuesday
Adam Wilson
978-0-9965227-9-3

Gurls, They'll Never Take Us Alive
Matt Lydon
978-1-7337360-3-9

Brethren Hollow
Bill Hemmig
978-1-7337360-8-4

Helium
Adam Wilson
and Jeff Chin
978-1-7337360-5-3

The Legend of Dave Bradley
S Atzeni
978-1-7371758-8-9

The Path Home
A.J. Pelligrino
979-8-9868097-8-6

Showboi: Too Deep Too Care
Jimmy Cullen
979-8-9868097-6-2

Wund to Space
Rowan Kilduf
978-1-960869-06-7

W(h)ine & Cheese
S. Atzeni
978-1-960869-12-8

Brooklyn Family Album
Margaret Montet
Coming September 2024

Tales from the Scrapyard
Nicole Zamlout
Coming 2025

The Heart Decided to Move
Melanie Bell
Coming 2025

Find the whole series online at:
readfuriously.com/one

www.ingramcontent.com/pod-product-compliance
Lightning Source LLC
Chambersburg PA
CBHW060336310726
48976CB00007B/2580